TOM NICOLL

LEVEL UP!

BEAST BATTLES

ILLUSTRATED BY
ANJAN SARKAR

LITTLE TIGER

LONDON

LEVEL 1

"Max? You still alive?" I asked.

"I think so," he replied, sitting up and wiping drool off his glasses. "You?"

"Of course I am, I just asked you," I said.

"Oh yeah, right," he said. "Sorry, I wasn't thinking straight. Probably from being eaten."

It was a bit much to take in. Especially when the thing that had eaten you was the size of a large bunny. On the other hand,

Max and I had seen and experienced quite a lot of strange things recently. Ever since a machine my mum built had accidentally transported us into a video game, we'd flown in epic space battles, been catapulted across a world made of blocks, and helped improve countless virtual lives along the way. When you think about it, is being eaten by a harmless-looking fluffy animal really that odd?

Actually, yes. Yes, it is.

"It's surprisingly big in here, don't you think?" asked Max.

"You're right," I agreed, staring around the cavern that was the inside of the creature that had eaten us. The walls were soft and fleshy, and it was a bit like being inside a hollowed-out giant pink flan. "I guess we're in another game then. One involving creatures with huge appetites."

"No kidding," said Max, pointing at some of the other things the creature had snacked on. They included:

- a grandfather clock
- a STOP sign
- a variety of trees and assorted shrubbery
- a couch
- tyres of several different sizes
- a small boat
- an entire fish tank, complete with fish

"What's that thing there?" asked Max, pointing at a small round hole in the middle of all the junk. It was black and swirling and kind of gooey, like a really thick soup.

"I don't know," I admitted. "Could be a wall glitch.

Best not go near it."

Max nodded slowly. "How are we going to get out of here then?"

"YOU'RE NOT GOING ANYWHERE, SO PIPE DOWN ALREADY," a voice boomed.

Max and I looked around. "Who said that?" I asked.

"Who do you think?" replied the voice. It sounded female. "Me. The thing that ate you."

"You can hear us?" asked Max.

"Of course I can hear you," she said. "I'm right here."

"As you can hear us," I said, "you'd better just go

ahead and spit us out. Right now!"

The creature made a snorting sound that caused her insides to jiggle, almost knocking us over. "Or what?" She laughed.

"Or… Or…" I said, trying to think of something. "OK, I don't know what. But you should let us go."

"I'm afraid I disagree," she said.

"Disagree?" I repeated, stroking my chin, an idea starting to form. "That's it. Max, I've got it."

"You have?" he asked.

"We're basically her food, right?" I said. "And we're in disagreement. Now, what normally happens when food disagrees with someone?"

Max considered this for a moment. "They throw up. But Flo, that expression doesn't literally mean the person is arguing with their lunch."

I rolled my eyes. "Obviously I know that. But

the principle is the same. We're going to make her throw up."

"You wouldn't…" said the creature, though she didn't sound convinced.

"We'll have to disagree on that too," I said, as I started jumping around in her stomach. "Come on, Max."

Max joined me, flinging himself into the soft mushy walls as I repeatedly stomped on the floor. After half a minute or so of this there was a loud groaning noise.

"Ooooooh, please … stop!" said the creature. "I think I'm going to…"

There was a loud retch.

BLEEEEEUUUUU UUURRRRRRG GGGGHHHHHH!!!

Then another.

And another.

And then…

We shot
out into the bright
daylight and landed in
a crumpled heap on the
grass, covered in drool.
I ducked as the grandfather
clock flew past us.
"That's better," I said, getting to
my feet and wiping off the slobber as best I could.
I turned round, ready to give the creature a piece of
my mind. But when I saw it, I stopped. She was in
tears, her tiny yellow fluffy paws covering her eyes.

"Er… Are you all right?" asked Max.

"No," she admitted.

Max gave me a look that said, 'Yeah, I know she just ate us and we have every right to be angry but she's clearly going through something right now, so we should probably be the bigger people and see if we can help her.' He packed a lot into that look.

I sighed. "What's your name?"

"Hungrabun." She sniffed.

"I'm Flo and this is Max," I said. "You want to tell us what's wrong?"

"What's wrong?" repeated Hungrabun. "Oh, just my life's dream being destroyed, that's all."

"Your dream was to eat us?" asked Max, understandably confused.

"What? No! My dream is to compete in the Battles but that's never going to happen. You were comfort snacks, and I can't even get that right. I'm such a failure."

I decided to skip past the part about us being comfort snacks. "The Battles? What are they?"

She looked up at us in shock, her eyes red from rubbing and snot dangling from her tiny nose. "You new in town?" she asked.

"Something like that," Max said.

"The Battles are a tournament where creatures team up and compete against each other," said Hungrabun, her face brightening as she explained. "Sixteen teams of two, each creature bringing their  own unique abilities to the fight until only one team is left standing. I've been watching the Battles ever since I hatched. It's always been my dream to compete in them and now that I'm finally old enough it's not going to happen."

"Why not?" asked Max.

"Because I can't find anyone who wants to team up with me, and they don't let you enter as a single," she said. "You get overexcited and accidentally eat one or two potential teammates and suddenly word gets out and no one wants to be your partner. I coughed both of them back up but no one ever mentions that part, do they?"

I grabbed Max by the arm and pulled him to one side. "I've just figured out what game this is," I whispered. "It's Critter Clash."

A look of realization dawned on Max's face. "Of course!"

Critter Clash was one of those games that everyone knew about, even people like Max who weren't into games. Playgrounds were always full of kids, or 'creature coaches', discussing tactics or recounting glorious victories.

"I bet we have to help Hungrabun win the tournament to escape the game," I said.

Max nodded. "I think you're probably right."

"Help me?" sniffed Hungrabun. "But you don't look like creatures. You look more like … coaches. But no one's seen a coach in years."

"We are!" I said. "And we'd like to become yours."

"What does she mean no one's seen one in years?" asked Max.

"It's probably because Critter Clash is so popular they keep bringing out new versions," I whispered. "I got mine a couple of years ago but no one plays it any more and Mum won't let me get the new one because she says I've got enough games, which is ridiculous. How can anyone have enough games?"

"So what makes you qualified, exactly?" interrupted Hungrabun.

Max and I looked at each other. "Well, Max is really clever," I said. "He can come up with game plans and strategies and tactics, that kind of thing. And I can show you some awesome fighting moves."

"Oh yeah?" said Hungrabun. "Like what?"

"Like my Dropkick of Doom for starters," I said before launching myself into the air, feet first. Unfortunately I quickly discovered that doing the move while PLAYING a video game was a lot easier than doing the move while IN a video game. I landed on my back with a massive, embarrassing thud.

I looked up at Hungrabun, who didn't seem hugely impressed.

"Actually," said Max. "Flo is really good at making you do things you don't want to do."

I glared at him.

"But that's a good quality in a coach," he clarified, before adding under his breath, "Not always in a best friend, mind you…"

Hungrabun looked like she was giving the idea serious thought but then she just shrugged. "Even if I were to accept, weren't you listening earlier?" she asked. "The Battles are tag team only. I can't enter without a partner. And the tournament starts tonight!"

"What if we could find you a partner before then?" I asked. "Could we be your coaches?"

Hungrabun gave us a long look before holding out her little paw. "Deal."

LEVEL 2

There was no time to waste. The tournament kicked off in a few hours, so we were going to have to work fast to find Hungrabun a partner. Unfortunately, as we traipsed through the cartoon-like forest, with its overly bright and colourful plant life, it was proving difficult to find anyone at all.

"These woods are normally full of creatures," explained Hungrabun after what felt like hours of wandering around. "But they'll have headed into town for the start of the tournament, to get the best seats. There's no one left here."

"I think our ideal teammate would be someone who's huge, with four arms and giant muscles," I said.

Hungrabun laughed. "Yeah, good luck finding a creature like that."

"There's one over there," I said, pointing towards the creature I had just described. It was green and huge – twice the size of me or Max – and it had a mean expression and looked like it was made for fighting, even though currently it was sitting on a tree stump looking bored. It was perfect!

"Finally!" said Max. "Nice work, Flo."

"Actually, Flo…" Hungrabun started to say, but I rushed over to introduce myself.

"Hi, I'm Flo," I said to the green creature. "And that's my friend Max over there. Has anyone ever told you you'd be perfect for fighting in the Battles?"

The creature stared at me, a confused expression forming painfully slowly on its face. Finally it said, "Wot?"

"Seriously, look at you," I said. "Your size, your muscles, that terrifying face you're making right now – you'd be amazing at it. My friend, the one hiding behind my other friend's leg right now, for some reason … she's called Hungrabun and she's going to be in the Battles too. Oh, she might look like the kind of fluffy toy you'd get free with an Easter egg but trust me, she's a warrior. I think you two could be a dream team. What do you say?"

The giant beast scratched its head. "Wot?"

"Um… Shall we start again? What's your name?" I asked, wondering if I had jumped in too quickly.

Then there came a voice that made my skin crawl. "His name's Guggernaut."

A weedy-looking rodent stepped out from behind a tree. He had a body like a rat's but longer, like a weasel's. He did not look best pleased.

"What's going on here?" he demanded.

"Hey, Pheasel," said Guggernaut, proving he actually did know words other than 'wot'. "This one wants me to join their team."

Pheasel looked like he was going to explode. "What? I nip to the little creatures' room for one minute and someone tries to steal MY teammate."

I held up my hands. "Hey, sorry, I didn't know he was already in a team."

"You haven't heard of the legendary Pheasel and Guggernaut?" asked Pheasel, looking doubtful.

"I have," said Hungrabun as she and Max joined me. "Big fan, by the way."

I frowned at her. "You might have said something."

"I tried to," she said. "But you ran off before I could."

"Let me enlighten you," continued Pheasel. "We are the reigning, defending, undefeated Battle Champions. No one can beat us, and no one will ever break us up either. Especially not to join something that looks like it got stuck inside a tumble dryer."

"Hey!" said Hungrabun, running a paw through her fur defensively.

"Guggernaut, why don't you give them a demonstration of our powers," said Pheasel, grinning a malicious grin.

"Sure thing, boss," said Guggernaut, standing up and cracking the knuckles on all four of his hands. Before we could react, he grabbed the three of us and started juggling us in the air.

"Hey, put us down!" I yelled.

"You heard her," said Pheasel. "Put them down."

Guggernaut obliged, launching us into the air. We flew above the forest for several seconds before crashing back down into some bushes.

"Well," I said as we pulled ourselves out. "I did not care for those two."

Hungrabun let out a long sigh. "I guess it's

probably for the best that we can't find anyone," she said. "I mean, even if we did, we'd never be able to beat Guggernaut."

"Oh, I wouldn't say that…"

The three of us turned our heads in different directions, trying to find the source of the voice. But there was no one there.

LEVEL 3

"Who said that?" asked Max.

"The creature that's going to win the Battles for you," came the reply from somewhere behind us. Or maybe it was in front of us, it was hard to tell.

"Show yourself," I said.

"But I am," the creature replied, even though it definitely wasn't. "I am the master of hiding. All but invisible. They seek me here, they seek me there, but they never find me. I'm a ghost, I'm the wind, I'm the change down the back of the couch. I'm—"

"There he is, behind that tree," said Hungrabun,

pointing towards an old oak.

A fluorescent-blue bird-like creature, not much bigger than Hungrabun, stepped into the clearing. "You spotted me," it said. "Well done! I'm incredibly hard for most people to see, you know. Sometimes I go weeks without anyone noticing me."

"Are you sure they're not just ignoring you?" asked Hungrabun.

The creature considered this then shook its head. "Nope. It's because I'm so good at hiding. My name's Kiwi."

"I'm Flo, this is Max and that's Hungrabun," I replied.

He held out a wing for us that Max and I shook but Hungrabun pretended she didn't see, in a way that made it clear she did. Kiwi didn't seem bothered though.

"Nice to meet you all," he said. "So, should we head into the city? We don't want to be late for the tournament."

"Whoa there, mister," said Hungrabun. "I haven't agreed to team up with you yet."

Kiwi looked puzzled. "Didn't you? I thought you did."

Hungrabun folded her arms. "Nope."

"Do you want to agree quickly, then we can go?" said Kiwi.

Hungrabun's jaw hit the floor. "What… I mean … you can't be… Agree???"

"Great," said Kiwi, smiling. "Glad to be on board."

An exasperated Hungrabun held up a paw. "No!" she shouted. "I'm not agreeing! Why would I want you on my team? What can you even do? Besides get on my nerves?"

Kiwi continued to smile, as if he hadn't noticed Hungrabun's hostility. "I told you," he said. "Hiding."

Hungrabun looked at us, dumbfounded. "Hiding?" she said. "How is hiding going to help in a battle?"

"If they can't find you, they can't hurt you," said Kiwi, tapping the side of his head as if he'd said something extremely clever.

"Yeah, but you can't hurt them either," yelled Hungrabun in disbelief. "Not if you're hiding."

"Er… Maybe Kiwi has other powers," suggested Max, sounding hopeful.

Kiwi shook his head. "No, just the hiding."

"Yes, well, thank you," said Hungrabun. "I think we'll pass."

"Actually, Kiwi," I said, putting an arm round Hungrabun. "Could you give us a few minutes?"

Kiwi nodded. "Sure. I'll just practise my hiding."

As Kiwi hurried off into the bushes, Hungrabun buried her face in her paws. "Can you believe that guy?" she moaned.

Max and I exchanged awkward glances.

Hungrabun noticed. "What?" she asked. "You're not actually thinking..."

"He's our only option," I said.

Max agreed. "If you want to be in the tournament, we're going to have to go with him."

Hungrabun wasn't convinced. "We could find someone else. We still have time."

"Besides Guggernaut and Pheasel, he's the only

person we've met," I said.

"And he hasn't attacked us … yet," added Max. "What about we have a little training session with Kiwi? See what he can do."

"Like … an audition?" asked Hungrabun.

"Exactly," said Max. "And if he's no good, we'll keep looking."

Hungrabun considered this. "Fine," she said. "But it'll be a waste of time."

"Great!" I said. I turned back towards where Kiwi had been, and no longer was. "Kiwi!"

"Yes, Flo?" he said, appearing next to me.

"Arrgh!" I cried, almost jumping out of my digital skin. "Don't sneak up on people like that."

"Sorry," he said. "It's a habit from hiding all the time. So, I heard you want us to train against each other. I was eavesdropping. It's another habit from hiding."

"That's all right," said Max. "Let's see what you've got."

"Or not see," said Kiwi. He pointed behind us. "Hey, is that Guggernaut?"

Hungrabun, Max and I spun round in terror, but there was no one there. I slapped my forehead and turned back. Kiwi, of course, had gone.

"A cheap trick," said Hungrabun dismissively, slowly scanning the clearing.

"But a good one," said Kiwi. "It almost always works... Arrgh!"

Without warning, Hungrabun somersaulted through the air then devoured Kiwi in a single bite.

She rubbed her paws together with glee, before spitting him back out.

"How did you spot him?" I asked. "I couldn't see him anywhere."

"I didn't see him, I heard him," she said. "What use is hiding if you're going to talk all the time?"

"Good point," said Kiwi. "Let's go again. But this time you won't hear a peep from me. Just give me a minute to wipe off all this drool."

From somewhere deep in his feathers, he removed a small towel. After giving himself a good dry, he held the towel up over himself then let it drop. It hit the ground, but Kiwi was gone.

"Oooh, magic," I said.

"Where'd he go this time?" asked Max, looking all around.

Hungrabun remained still, holding up her right paw. She sniffed the air a few times, then turned round on the spot and took another massive chomp, swallowing Kiwi once more. For the second time, she spat him out in a heap.

"How?" I asked.

"I could smell him," she said. "Smell is a very important part of taste, you know. Being a big foodie, my senses of taste and smell are excellent."

"OK, another go," said Kiwi, grabbing his towel again.

"No…" said Hungrabun, but Kiwi was already out of sight. Hungrabun rolled her eyes and started sniffing again. After a few seconds, she winced and covered her nose. Moments later Max and I grabbed our noses too.

"Did you fart?" yelled Hungrabun.

"That's gross!" said Max.

"Bet you won't want to follow my scent now," said Kiwi from somewhere.

"That's it, I'm done," said Hungrabun, storming past me and Max.

"Come on," I protested. "Even you have to admit that was pretty clever. Disgusting, but clever."

"You can't expect me to team up with him," she said. "Hiding and farting aren't going to help us win anything. We need to find someone else."

Max and I looked at each other. "She might be right," he sighed.

"Hey, Hungrabun," said Kiwi. "I was just wondering, now that we're a team…"

Hungrabun threw her paws up in the air. "Now that we're a team?"

"Exactly," said Kiwi. "I was wondering whose

Battle Coin you wanted to use to enter the tournament?"

There was a long pause. Hungrabun seemed to have frozen, her paws still in the air. Eventually she said in a low voice, "Battle … Coin?"

"Yeah, you know, the coin they gave you after you registered for the tournament," he said matter-of-factly. "Every team has to cash in one for entry. Should we use yours or mine? I suppose it's good that we have a spare. That'll mean at least one of those teams on the waiting list will get to compete. Those poor guys, I'd hate to be in their shoes, forgetting to get their paperwork in early. Everyone knows you need to apply at least a year in advance to have a chance of getting in."

A wide-eyed Hungrabun seemed to have lost the colour in her face all of a sudden. We both turned to look at her.

"You did remember to register for the tournament, didn't you?" Max whispered to her.

"Not exactly…" she replied.

"Right." I said. "So if you want to compete, it's basically Kiwi or …"

"… nothing," she finished.

Another few seconds of silence passed.

"Well?" I asked her.

Hungrabun stared at the ground. "I think we should use your coin, Kiwi," she said.

A grinning Kiwi appeared right next to us, making us all jump.

"But you have to stop doing that," said Hungrabun.

LEVEL 4

With the start of the tournament rapidly approaching, the four of us set off into the city. Critter Clash had always been a big deal to the kids who played it in the real world but that was nothing compared to the sense of occasion we could feel in the game itself, as thousands of creatures of all shapes, sizes and colours filled the streets. Giant billboard displays hyped up the tournament, showing highlight reel clips from previous Beast Battles.

"Welcome to Fight City," yelled Kiwi over the noise of the crowds as we squeezed our way past what looked like an elephant crossed with a butterfly.

I glanced up just in time to see a clip of Guggernaut stacking two creatures on top of each other before flattening them both. Then Pheasel's weaselly face filled the screen while his voice boomed out, "We're Pheasel and Guggernaut and there's no one who can stop us. Only a fool would try. If you knew what was good for you, all you other teams would stay at home."

"Chance would be a fine thing," I heard Max muttering behind me.

"I think we're in there," said Kiwi, gesturing to the entrance of a massive domed arena.

Hungrabun's eyes lit up. "The Brawlosseum! I've dreamed of competing there my entire life."

We made our way through the masses until we reached the entrance. What looked like a bull wearing a suit put up a hoof to stop us.

"Sorry, folks," he said. "The stadium's not open to spectators yet."

"Oh, we're not spectators," said Kiwi, pulling out a small golden coin with a fist engraved on it.

The bull looked at the coin, then at Kiwi, then at the coin again, then at Kiwi. This went on for some time. "You're competing in the tournament?"

"That's right, my good sir," said Kiwi proudly.

"Wow," said the bull. "Really? Wow! You must have some amazing powers to want to compete in a tournament against Guggernaut."

"He's really good at hiding," said Hungrabun.

The bull screwed up his face. "Hiding? That's not a power."

"Don't get me started," sighed Hungrabun.

"Can we get in then?" I asked, trying to move the conversation away from how likely we were to lose.

The bull pulled out a small tablet from his jacket and swiped a few times. "What's the team name?" he asked.

"Super Fluffy Animals," beamed Kiwi.

"What?" said Hungrabun. "That is not our name."

"Super Fluffy Animals," said the bull. "Here you are. In you go. Good luck – you'll need it."

"Thank you," said Kiwi, marching through the entrance.

"Can we change that name?" Hungrabun asked the bull.

"Nope," he said. "All team names are final upon registration."

Hungrabun folded her arms and walked into the building. "Can't believe I forgot to register," I heard her muttering.

*

Halfway down the corridor inside we were greeted by a creature that looked mostly like a gorilla, except for the giant tortoise shell on its back.

"Super Fluffy Animals, I presume?" she said. "I was beginning to think you weren't going to show. Looking at you, I'm surprised you did. Anyway, my name's Shilla. I'm the tournament co-ordinator."

"Nice to meet you," said Kiwi.

"I'm sure," she said. "Battle Coin?"

Kiwi handed over the gold coin. Shilla inspected

it, turning it over a few times and even biting it. Satisfied that it was genuine, she nodded and said, "Follow me."

She led us down the corridor until we came to a door with the number sixteen written on it. "Every team gets a dressing room," she said, opening the door to reveal a small room with, among other things, a battered couch, a TV and a whiteboard. Shilla turned to me and Max and looked us up and down. "You two … you're coaches?"

"That's right," I said.

"Hmm. Not seen many of you for a while," she said, reaching an arm up behind the door and pulling two jackets from a hook. She brushed them with her hand, knocking dust to the floor. She tossed one to each of us. "Coaches' jackets. You need to wear these at all times."

"Cool," said Max. They were blue and red, with large white letter Cs emblazoned on the back.

"Not the word I would use to describe them," I said, slipping mine on.

Shilla handed us a slip of paper. "These are the brackets for the tournament," she said. "As I'm sure you know, it's sixteen teams in a knockout format. You lose, you're eliminated, you go home. If you can, that is."

I swallowed a lump in my throat. Shilla was talking about the creatures competing, but for me and Max, her words about going home took on a whole different meaning…

"If you win," continued Shilla, "then you advance to the next round. You'll need to win four matches in total to win the tournament."

We looked at the brackets:

CRITTER CLASH

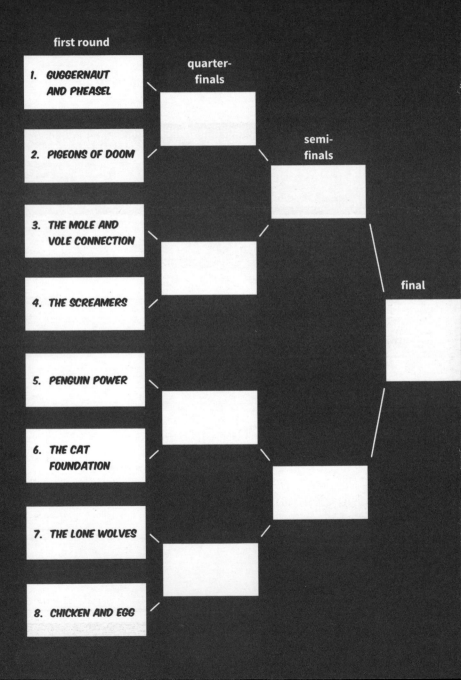

first round

quarter-finals

semi-finals

final

1. GUGGERNAUT AND PHEASEL

2. PIGEONS OF DOOM

3. THE MOLE AND VOLE CONNECTION

4. THE SCREAMERS

5. PENGUIN POWER

6. THE CAT FOUNDATION

7. THE LONE WOLVES

8. CHICKEN AND EGG

TOURNAMENT

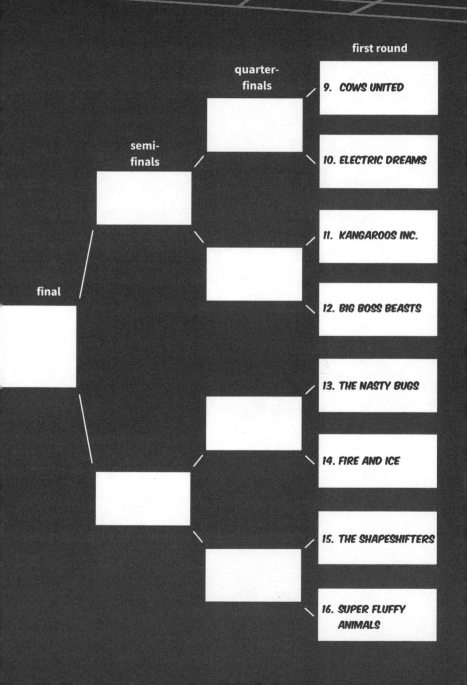

first round

quarter-finals

semi-finals

final

9. COWS UNITED

10. ELECTRIC DREAMS

11. KANGAROOS INC.

12. BIG BOSS BEASTS

13. THE NASTY BUGS

14. FIRE AND ICE

15. THE SHAPESHIFTERS

16. SUPER FLUFFY ANIMALS

"The Shapeshifters?" I said. "They any good?"

"Semi-finalists last year," said Hungrabun. "So, yeah – they're OK."

Max switched on the TV. "Better start trying to come up with a strategy to beat them then," he said.

"I'll help," said Hungrabun.

"Not right now you won't," said Shilla. "We need promo videos from you two. We should have had them filmed hours ago, but you decided to be late."

"Promo videos?" I asked.

"Yeah, you know," said Shilla. "They introduce themselves, tell everyone how they're going to beat the other teams, get the crowds hyped up. That kind of thing."

"Great. We'll do that and leave Max to strategize," I said.

Shilla led us to another room where a bearlike

creature was waiting with a camera pointed at a large green screen.

"Oh man, this is awesome," said Kiwi, jumping about excitedly.

I could tell from the panicked expression on Hungrabun's face that she didn't agree. "Er… You mean, I have to speak into that?" she asked, pointing at the camera.

"That's generally how it works, sweetie, yes," Shilla said as she shuffled Hungrabun in front of the green screen. "You can go first."

"Hang on…" said Hungrabun.

The bear pushed a button on the camera then said, "Three, two, one, go!"

Hungrabun's eyes somehow grew even bigger. "Er… H-h-hi…" she stammered. "My … my name is Hungrabun … and … I'm-er-I'm-er-I'm-er…"

"Is she stuck on a loop?" whispered Shilla.

"What my partner's trying to say," said Kiwi, stepping in. "Is that she's a lean, mean, eating machine and no team can stop her jaws of justice from devouring them. And I'm Kiwi, the master of stealth. Don't bother looking for me: you won't find me, except in your nightmares. Because we're the Super Fluffy Animals and we're coming for everyone. And, Guggernaut and Pheasel, if you two are listening, we're not scared of you. You don't impress us. Everyone's talking about you as if you're unbeatable. But once this tournament is over, no one's going to be talking about you, period. The only thing anyone will be talking about is the Super Fluffy Animals running wild. That's all we've got to say about that."

Everyone in the room stared at Kiwi in stunned silence.

"That. Was. Amazing," said Shilla, turning to the camera bear. "Did you get all that?"

"Sure did," he said, tapping the camera.

Shilla looked at her watch. "Perfect," she said. "The tournament will be starting soon so you'd better get back to your dressing room. They'll call you once the matches have begun. Good luck. Although if you can fight as well as you can talk, perhaps you won't need it."

Outside in the corridor, Hungrabun glared at Kiwi. "I didn't need you to speak for me."

Kiwi grinned sheepishly. "Sorry… I got a little carried away there."

49

"That was pretty great though," I said. "I had goosebumps."

"Thanks, Flo," said Kiwi. "I don't know where it all came from. I just saw the red light on the camera and it spilled out of me."

"There's just one thing…" I said.

Kiwi nodded. "Yeah? Tell me, I love constructive feedback. Well, I imagine I do. Technically I've never actually had any before, but I'm sure it's awesome."

I shook my head. "No, it's not criticism," I said. "I just wondered … what Guggernaut and Pheasel will think when they see it."

Kiwi opened his mouth, then closed it again. "Oh. That's right. They'll see all that, won't they?"

Hungrabun groaned. "They're going to kill us."

For the first time since we'd met him, the smile vanished from Kiwi's face.

LEVEL 5

We returned to the dressing room to find it a mess. Sheets of paper littered every square inch of the room. I thought someone had been in and trashed the place until I spotted Max in among the piles, scrawling all over the whiteboard with a pen.

"… carry the one…" he muttered, before spotting us. "Ah, you're back."

"Max, what's this?" I asked.

Max looked around as if he hadn't noticed. "Oh, this? Just some notes I've made on the Shapeshifters. You know, statistical breakdowns, performance reviews, in-depth profiles, that kind of thing."

"How long were we away?" asked Kiwi, pushing his way through the room.

Hungrabun picked up several sheets of paper. "Are we supposed to read all this?"

Max looked around at the mess then burst out laughing. "This?" he said. "Don't be silly."

Kiwi and Hungrabun looked visibly relieved.

"I've still got loads more to do," said Max. "This only covers a couple of the Shapeshifters' matches."

The Super Fluffy Animals' faces dropped.

"Er... Max," I said, stepping in and taking a seat on a big pile of paper. "You can't expect them to read all this. It's a bit much. They just need a few useful tips to help them win. Like you get in those gaming videos online."

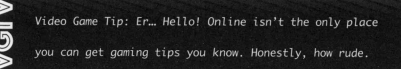
VGTV

Video Game Tip: Er... Hello! Online isn't the only place you can get gaming tips you know. Honestly, how rude.

"A few useful tips?" repeated Max, thinking to himself. "I suppose you could read the Quick Summary I wrote about them."

"Cool, that sounds perfect," I said. "Where's that then?"

"You're sitting on it," he said.

I looked down at the paper seat beneath me. "Not quite what I was hoping for," I said. "Look, just tell us their strengths and weaknesses."

Max nodded. "OK. The Shapeshifters' biggest strength is the fact that they've been teaming up for years, so they're a well-oiled machine."

Hungrabun nodded. "They were in the first Battles I ever watched," she said. "They're legends."

"And unlike most teams," continued Max, "that

normally consist of team members with different but complementary skills, the Shapeshifters have identical powers. As their name suggests, they can take other forms. Last year, they turned into campervans and ran over their opposition to win a match. So… I guess look out for that."

I pointed at Hungrabun and Kiwi. "Watch out for campervans, or any vehicles really," I said. "See, this is useful stuff. What about weaknesses then?"

"None," said Max.

I nodded. "Right. So… Wait a minute. What do you mean none?"

"Well, none yet I mean," he said. "They won all the matches I've watched. Easily."

Kiwi and Hungrabun were looking more and more nervous by the second. Coaches are meant to build up their team's confidence and so far, Max and I didn't seem to be doing a great job of that.

There was a knock on the door, almost drowned out by a giant roar coming from the arena. Shilla popped her head into the room. "Just to let you know, that's the first match under way. You'll be called once it's your turn." And with that, she slammed the door.

"Oh no," said Hungrabun. "We haven't even got a plan. We're going to lose. This was a horrible mistake."

"Come on," said Kiwi. "Think positive."

"I'm positive this was a horrible mistake," said Hungrabun.

I knew I had to do something. And with the tournament starting we didn't have much time. But I had an idea.

"You two, follow me," I said. "Max, you stay here

and find some holes in the Shapeshifters' game."

"I'll try my best," he shouted as I left the room, Hungrabun and Kiwi scurrying after me.

"Where are we going?" asked Hungrabun.

"To get some inspiration," I said.

I'd been worried that finding our way through the arena would be difficult, but fortunately all I had to do was follow the racket.

The crowd was in full swing by the time we arrived at the team entranceway. Even backstage the noise was deafening. I could see several other teams watching the action from behind the curtains. I found us a spot away from them and pulled a section open, letting the three of us peek into the arena.

Kiwi and Hungrabun's eyes lit up with excitement as they stuck their heads through the curtains.

"I thought this might help settle your nerves,"

I said. "You know, get used to the arena before you go out there. Take in a few matches, maybe get some ideas for your own match."

"Great idea, Flo," said Kiwi. "This is awesome."

I pushed my own head through the curtain. The arenas in Critter Clash all had different themes.

The Brawlosseum was modelled on the old Roman gladiator arenas with stone seating and marble columns. It was currently filled with tens of thousands of creatures dressed

PIGEONS OF DOOM

in togas, cheering or booing, fixated on the centre of the arena or on giant video screens, where they could watch two teams going head to head on a round platform.

To be more accurate, one member of one team was going head to head with both members of the other. Guggernaut had a pigeon-like creature in one hand, and a second pigeon-like creature in another. He was repeatedly bashing their heads together, while pulling bodybuilder-like flexes with his other two arms. I could see Pheasel laughing and urging Guggernaut on at the edge of the platform.

After at least a minute of this, Pheasel held his rat thumb out then turned it upside down, at which point Guggernaut launched the creatures into the stands.

A bell rang and the match was over.

"Wow," said Kiwi. "That Guggernaut's tough. I really wouldn't want to get on the wrong side of him."

A cat wearing a tuxedo and holding a microphone jumped on to the platform. "Ladies and gentlebeasts, your winners, and advancing to the quarter-finals – Guggernaut and Pheasel."

"It's Pheasel and Guggernaut," corrected Pheasel, grabbing the mic. "And what you all saw right there was just a small taste of what's to come for those other fools in the back. There's not a team alive who can beat me ... I mean us." Pheasel tossed the microphone back to the announcer.

"Funny you should say that, Pheasel," said the cat. "It seems not everyone agrees with you."

The large video screens switched to an image of

two creatures I recognized.

"Hey, that's us!" said Kiwi.

"Oh no," groaned Hungrabun.

The video they had recorded earlier, where Kiwi had said a few things about Guggernaut and Pheasel, played in its entirety. For the benefit of people who wouldn't know who Kiwi and Hungrabun were, their names were helpfully listed underneath their pictures.

After the video finished, two things happened.

One was expected: Guggernaut and Pheasel hit the roof. This didn't escape the notice of the announcer, who quickly got out of there.

The second thing was less expected: the crowd erupted. They had been noisy before but it had been nothing compared to this. Chants started breaking out:

"Wow!" said Kiwi. "They love us. They've even taken the initials of Super Fluffy Animals to turn it into an easy-to-yell chant. That's the sign of a popular team."

"Yeah, but look how angry we've made Guggernaut and Pheasel," said Hungrabun.

Kiwi shrugged. "So what? We'll have to face them at some point if we're going to win," he said. "But with a crowd like that behind us, no one can stop us."

Hungrabun took another look at the crowd, still chanting their names. "I hope you're right," she said.

So did I.

LEVEL 6

We had only just returned to our dressing room when there was a knock on the door.

"It's time," said Shilla.

"Right, team, this is it," I said.

The four of us left the dressing room and began the long march down the corridor, Kiwi and Hungrabun in front, me and Max following them. Max was quickly trying to describe what he had found about our opponents, the Shapeshifters.

"Changing shape takes it out of them a little," he explained, glancing down at the large pile of paper in his arms. "So, the best time to strike is immediately after they've taken a new form."

There was no response from Hungrabun or Kiwi.

"Guys, did you hear me?" asked Max.

"They heard you," I said. "They're just getting in the zone. This is what I'm like, right before I play in a game tournament. You have to tune everything out and just visualize yourself winning. It's quite easy for me because, as you know, I'm the greatest gamer of all time."

"Right," said Max, rolling his eyes.

We reached the entrance to the arena.

"OK, team, here we go," I said. "You got this."

We stepped into the arena and once again the place exploded.

"Wow… You weren't kidding when you said they liked Kiwi's video," Max yelled into my ear.

It was a long walk to the centre and while

Hungrabun seemed to be doing her best to keep her nerves together, Kiwi was in his element, high-fiving creatures as he passed, signing autographs and even taking selfies with them.

We reached the platform where the Shapeshifters were waiting for us on the opposite side. Their current form, perhaps their natural one, reminded me of two jellyfish, except they were larger, luminous-green and wearing sparkly purple masks with yellow stars over the eyes.

"I wish we had cool outfits," said Kiwi as he and Hungrabun jumped up on to the platform. Max and I took our positions in the coaching area just behind them on the outside of the ring, marked by a white box on the arena floor.

A zebra wearing a somewhat pointless black and white striped shirt was standing in the middle of the platform.

"Must be the ref," I said to Max.

Then the tuxedo-wearing cat-announcer stepped in. "Ladies and gentlebeasts, it's time!" his voice boomed out. "The following contest will be one round with no time limit. Introducing first, in the blue corner … they hail from Parts Unknown with a combined weight of … well, it varies … Morpher and Camo – the Shapeshifters!"

"How can there be corners when the ring's a circle?" asked Max.

"Really?" I said. "That's what you're most worried about right now?"

"I'm not worried … just making an observation," he grumbled.

"And their opponents in the red corner …"

I could hear Max tutting.

"… from deep in the heart of the jungle, making their Battles debut, with a combined weight equal to an orange, it's Hungrabun and Kiwi. They are the **SUPER! FLUFFY! ANIMALS!**"

"I want a good clean fight," yelled the ref, over the roars of the crowd. "One of you in at all times, the other stays in their corner until the tag. Any questions from either corner?"

Max put up his hand. I quickly pulled it down.

"You were going to ask about the corners, weren't you?" I asked.

"Maybe," said Max.

"OK, good," continued the ref. "Let's do this."

The bell rang.

"I'll go first," said Hungrabun.

"No worries," said Kiwi. "I got this."

"Kiwi, no, wait," cried Hungrabun, but Kiwi was already bouncing across the ring. Hungrabun put her head in her paws. "This is going to be a disaster."

Kiwi came face to face with what I think was Morpher. The green blob looked down at Kiwi with bemusement. He grinned up at her, holding out a wing to shake.

"Good luck to you," he said.

"And to you," said Morpher, a gelatinous hand

reaching out from the blob and taking hold of Kiwi's wing. After a few seconds Kiwi tried to remove his wing, but Morpher didn't let go. Instead, she sort of melded into her own hand. It expanded rapidly until Kiwi was shaking what looked like the detached hand of a giant.

The hand snatched Kiwi then proceeded to pound him against the ground.

"Kiwi!" the three of us yelled.

The hand went up again but just as it was about to drop, it paused. Slowly, the fist opened, revealing an empty palm. Kiwi wasn't there.

"Where'd he go?" asked Morpher. I decided not to think too much about how a giant hand would be able to talk. I preferred leaving those kind of thoughts to Max.

"Over there," yelled Camo, pointing behind her.

A dazed Kiwi was crawling towards our corner.

"Kiwi, tag me in," shouted Hungrabun, stretching her tiny arm out as far as it could go, which wasn't that far. Any hope that Kiwi would make it quickly vanished when the giant hand grabbed him and tossed him casually towards the Shapeshifters' corner. Morpher then tagged in Camo, who changed into a huge mallet. Morpher as a giant hand grabbed the mallet and swung it towards Kiwi, who barely rolled out of the way in time to avoid being flattened.

"Come on, ref!" I yelled. "It's two on one, get him out of there."

Hungrabun had seen enough. She rushed across the ring but had only got halfway when the ref stepped in and grabbed her. "Hey, back to your corner," he yelled.

"Come on!" she yelled back. "What about them?"

"Out!"

The crowd booed the referee as Hungrabun was left with no choice but to retreat to her corner. With the ref's back still turned, the Shapeshifters continued to play whack-a-Kiwi.

Morpher raised the hammer again, then … nothing. She just stood there.

"Hey, you two," shouted the ref, finally deciding to get involved. "Morpher, out!"

Morpher still didn't move. Her grip on Camo loosened, dropping her on to the mat. But Camo too seemed to be frozen.

"What's going on?" I asked Max.

"I'm not sure," he said

The Shapeshifters seemed to flicker for a second, then Morpher turned on the spot, the index finger of her giant fist extending so that she was pointing.

"Is she pointing at me?" asked Hungrabun.

Meanwhile, Camo had turned herself into a giant arrow, also pointing directly towards Hungrabun.

"You want a piece of me, is that it?" asked Hungrabun. "Kiwi, get over here."

"Gladly," moaned Kiwi, rolling across the mat and making the tag, to huge approval from the crowd.

"Hungrabun, wait," shouted Max as he quickly flicked through his notes. "It could be a trap. I can't find anything in their history like this."

"You said the best time to strike was just after they'd changed," yelled Hungrabun. "That suits me!"

She dived through the air then brought her jaws down on Morpher, swallowing her whole. She turned to Camo, the giant arrow still pointing right at her, even as she moved across the floor. Another bite and Camo was gone.

The bell rang.

The crowd erupted.

It was over.

Max and I rushed into the ring, a still-woozy Kiwi following us.

"Hungrabun, you did it!" I yelled.

The ring announcer reappeared. "Your winners, and moving on to the quarter-finals …" he boomed.

"… THE SUPER FLUFFY ANIMALS!"

As S-F-A chants broke out, I looked at Hungrabun. Had her face always been green?

LEVEL 7

"I'm just a little bloated, that's all," said Hungrabun
as the dune buggy arrived at our next destination
– a tropical beach, complete with golden sands,
luscious green palm trees and glistening turquoise
water. Brawl Beach had always been one of my
favourite arenas in the game. It had a more laid-
back feel than the Brawlosseum, though it seemed
unlikely that we were in for a relaxing time.

"You look ill," I said as the four of us got out.

"I'll be fine," she said. "Just need to walk it off
before the next round."

Shilla, wearing a sarong and flip-flops, met us and directed us to our new changing room – a beachside tent. Despite the location, inside it was kitted out exactly like our previous changing room, including the same TV, couch and whiteboard.

"We'll be ready for you soon," Shilla said, walking away. "So you might want to hurry over to the Power Stand and get your upgrades now."

"Upgrades?" asked Max.

"I totally forgot about those!" shrieked a recovered Kiwi, clapping his feathers together.

"So did I!" I said. "This is great. After every win you get a free credit to choose an upgrade."

"You mean, new skills and abilities?" said Max.

"Exactly," said Kiwi. "Or items. Ooh, look, there's the stand just there. Let's go."

The four of us followed Kiwi across the

sand to what looked like a burger van. Inside was a menu board that, instead of offering food, promised things like health and stamina upgrades. A bored panda looked down at us.

"What'll it be?" she asked.

"Kiwi, we're extremely … hic … underpowered," said Hungrabun, holding a paw to her mouth as though she might throw up any second. "So it's very … hic … important that we take the time to consider which upgrades would help us the most. We can't just … hic … rush into a decision. We need to think things through… What have you got on?"

"I got a new coat!" said Kiwi, giving us a turn in a shiny red puffer jacket. "Isn't it amazing? Seriously, how cool do I look right now?"

"A coat?" yelled Hungrabun. "Are you kidding me?"

"Now, Hungrabun," I said trying to calm her down. "Perhaps the coat has armour or something?"

The panda shook her head. "No, it's just a coat. Looks good though."

"It does look good," agreed Kiwi.

"No exchanges," added the panda.

Hungrabun sighed what was becoming a familiar sigh. "I guess it's left to me to save the team, again," she said, scanning the menu. "Give me a health vial. Those are actually useful."

"You want a red one or a blue one?" asked the panda. "Red ones restore up to seventy-per-cent health but you can only use them on yourself. Blue ones restore up to forty-per-cent health but you can use them on your partner if you want."

"You mean he blows his credit on a jacket and I have to bail him out with my health vial?" Hungrabun looked insulted. "I don't think so. Give me the red one."

"Maybe you should use it now," I suggested. She was looking worse by the second.

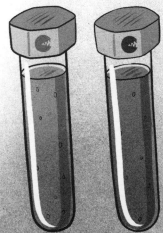

"I'm all right," she said. "Here, you hold on to it for me."

I slipped the vial into the pocket of my jacket as Hungrabun stared intently at something. I followed her gaze to a giant TV screen, where Guggernaut and Pheasel were engaged in their quarter-final match. I say engaged: Pheasel seemed to be looking at his phone while Guggernaut pounded a mole and a vole into submission. It was over in seconds.

The four of us said nothing but I knew we were all thinking the same thing. How was anyone going to beat Guggernaut?

That was a problem for another time though. We had our next team to focus on – Fire and Ice. As we walked back to our tent, I asked Max, "What's our game plan?"

Max didn't seem to hear me.

"Max?"

He turned to me. "Oh, sorry," he said. "I was just thinking about the Shapeshifters. I don't understand why they stopped fighting like that."

"I don't know," I said. "Maybe a bug?"

Video Game Tip: A bug as in a glitch in the game, not a bug like an insect. You probably knew that but I point it out because, let's be honest, in this game that could easily be one of the participants.

"Maybe," agreed Max. "I was thinking though, what about the people actually playing the game in the real world? What if someone was controlling the team at the time?"

"Then we'd have seen them in the opposing coaches' area. But no one plays this version of the game any more," I pointed out. "Now we need a plan for the next match. I've been thinking, one of the things I picked up about this game … er … I mean sport … in my years of playing … um … coaching is that it's important to keep tagging in regularly. It helps preserve the team's energy and it also keeps your opponents on their toes."

"Can't Hungrabun just eat them again?" asked Max.

"I don't think—" I began.

"Sure I can," said Hungrabun. "You can count on me."

"You really don't look that great," said Kiwi. "Maybe I should take the lead on this one?"

Hungrabun blurted out a laugh. "You and your coat?" she said. "Look, I know you're trying, Kiwi, but we need to stick to what we're good at. Some of us are cut out to be fighters, and some of us … aren't."

For the first time since I met him, the optimism had vanished from Kiwi's face. Even Hungrabun noticed it.

"Don't be like that," she said. "We just need to play to our strengths, that's all. Leave the fighting to me. I've got this."

✳

She didn't have it. When the match came round, Hungrabun insisted on starting. As soon as the bell rang she rushed at Ignita, a miniature red dragon, and brought her jaws down on the creature's tail.

And then proceeded to nibble at it, like a baby sucking on a pacifier.

"What's she doing?" Max asked.

Ignita seemed to be asking the same question, giving her partner Frostin, a polar bear made from ice, a look of total confusion. Meanwhile the crowd, seated on wooden stands surrounding the ring, was getting bored. Many of them were choosing to entertain themselves by passing around beach balls. Well, I think they were beach balls. They could have been creatures that looked like beach balls.

"She's too full to eat anything," I said. "But she's

too stubborn to give up."

As Hungrabun continued weakly trying to eat Ignita's tail, the dragon decided she'd had enough. Her tail suddenly glowed bright orange. Hungrabun sprang away, clasping at her mouth.

"HOT HOT HOT!!!" she yelled, fanning at her mouth with her paws.

Ignita followed that up by blowing a barrage of fireballs, forcing Hungrabun to fall back to our corner, luckily with only minimal singeing of her fur. Before Hungrabun had a chance to recover, Kiwi slapped her arm, tagging himself in.

"Hey, wait—" shouted Hungrabun, but the determined Kiwi wasn't about to change his mind.

"Do we at least have a strategy for him?" I asked Max hopefully.

"Try to stay alive?" said Max.

"I've seen you," Ignita said to Kiwi. "You talk a good game, but your last match showed you don't walk the walk. Maybe you just need someone to set a little fire underneath you."

A fiery blast landed at Kiwi's feet. Or at

least where they had been a second before. Because his feet, thankfully still attached to Kiwi himself, were now behind Ignita.

"You're fast, I'll give you that," Ignita acknowledged. "And you have a nice jacket."

"Thanks, and thanks," said Kiwi.

"But neither will save you," said Ignita, firing several fireballs in Kiwi's direction.

But again, Kiwi wasn't there.

"I'm over here," he said helpfully. Ignita spun round, annoyance written clearly on her face.

"You can't run all day," she hissed.

"You'd be surprised," said Kiwi.

"It's time to put you on ice," yelled a voice behind Kiwi. There was a thud as Kiwi was struck in the back. Frostin had snuck up behind him and now a sheet of ice extended from his paws to Kiwi's back, locking him in place.

"REF, COME ON!!!" Max, Hungrabun and I all yelled together.

As Kiwi tried unsuccessfully to move, Ignita smiled and said, "You're fired," before opening her jaws and exhaling a huge blast of fire.

Kiwi was a goner.

In that he was gone, I mean, not that he was dead.

In fact, he hadn't even gone that far. He stood next to Ignita, watching the dragon continue to blow fire at the spot where he'd just been standing. It took a good few seconds for Ignita to notice him. When she did, the fire from her breath petered out.

"Wh-what?" she stammered. "How?"

"I just took off my coat," said Kiwi casually, pointing to the charred remains of his red puffer jacket. "Don't think I'll be wearing it again. Hey, what happened to your friend?"

That's when we all saw it. Next to the jacket was a large puddle. Ignita let out a gasp and rushed towards it. "Frostin! My friend! Nooooooo!"

Kiwi walked over beside her. "I know how you feel," he said. "I loved that jacket."

He gave Ignita a sympathetic pat on the back. Unfortunately for Ignita, it was a little too hard and she went face first into the puddle. The water didn't seem to agree with the fiery dragon, judging by her screams and the steam rising off her. After a moment or two, Ignita had completely vanished.

The bell rang. The crowd exploded into cheers. Hungrabun, Max and I exchanged the same stunned looks.

We had won.

LEVEL 8

"Kiwi, that was incredible!" said Hungrabun when we got to the backstage area.

"Really?" said Kiwi. "I mostly just took off my jacket."

"The way you set them up like that, genius!" she said. "Using their powers against each other. I mean, thinking about it, I'm not sure how good an idea it is to be in a team where the other creature can accidentally kill you."

"Oh, they're not dead," said Shilla, pulling up in a dune buggy. "The medical team are pouring Frostin into a mould. A few days in the freezer, he'll be right as rain. Speaking of rain, Ignita should be turning into it soon, and then she'll turn back into her old form. Dragons are weird creatures. Anyway, jump in, we need to get you over to the next arena for the semi-finals."

Somehow, we were still in the tournament and still in with a shot of escaping the game. Our next opponents were Electric Dreams. They consisted of a toad-like creature called Flipswitch, who had an electric tongue, and a boar dressed in a cape and top hat. This was Hypnohog, who apparently was a master of hypnosis.

The arena at the beach had been hot but the new one was even worse. The stadium looked like it had been built from granite and rubble and it was surrounded by a moat of red-hot molten lava.

"The Brimstone Bowl," said Hungrabun as the buggy crossed a bridge into the arena. "We're in the middle of an active volcano."

"Is that safe?" asked Max.

"If you care about safety you don't sign up for the Battles," I replied.

"Well put," said Hungrabun.

Inside the Brimstone Bowl, we found ourselves once again in a familiar room complete with TV, couch and whiteboard.

"I'll be back later to bring you out," said Shilla. "So, just chill or train or whatever it is you creatures do when you're not fighting. Oh yes, I almost forgot – there's a stand just down the corridor where you can choose your new items."

"Ooh, let's go do that," said Kiwi.

Hungrabun didn't need any persuading.

"Those two seem to be getting on better at least," I said as they rushed off.

"Mmm," mumbled Max. He seemed distracted.

"You OK?" I asked.

"Sorry?" he said. "Oh yeah. I'm fine. I was just thinking about the Shapeshifters again."

"Still?" I said.

He nodded. "Something about how they glitched keeps nagging at me. I can't put my finger on it."

"Max," I said. "I once played a game where the car I was driving changed into a giant peanut."

Max squinted his eyes. "O-K," he said.

"My point is," I said. "These are video games. Bugs happen. No point in getting obsessed over them. We need to be concentrating on our next match. You know, so we can maybe get home."

"You're right," he said. "And we're not in for

an easy time. Electric Dreams are a dangerous combination."

"We'll just have to be more dangerous-er," I said. "What we really need are items to counter their shock attacks and hypnosis."

"Er… Right," agreed Max. "We should probably go tell the team that before Kiwi gets himself another useless jacket."

"To be fair," I said, closing the dressing-room door behind us. "Without the jacket we would have lost that match for sure. Maybe he does know what he's doing?"

We made our way down the corridor and quickly discovered that Kiwi hadn't bought himself a new coat.

"I got new trainers!" he shouted, pointing at his feet, which were now encased in a pair of white

sneakers with red
lightning bolts on
the sides.

Max and I frowned.
"Or maybe he doesn't
know what he's
doing," I said.

"Do they at least
make you go faster?"
asked Max.

"Nope," said Hungrabun, grinning. "They just
make him look cooler."

"Why didn't you stop him?" I asked.

Hungrabun shrugged. "He sacrificed his jacket
to win us the last match, so I figured he deserved
something nice. Besides, don't worry, I got us
something that might actually come in useful."

She held up a shiny metal shield.

"It's got plus ten defensive powers," she said.

Max looked at me blankly. "Is that good?"

"It's definitely better than a pair of trainers," I said. "Anyway, let's get back to the dressing room and figure out our game plan. I've got some ideas I want to write up on the whiteboard…"

We headed back along the corridor.

"That's weird," said Max, pointing at our door, which was wide open. "Didn't you close that?"

I narrowed my eyes. "Yeah, I did."

The four of us peered inside and let out a collective gasp.

"Someone's trashed the place!" I yelled.

The TV was smashed to smithereens, all that was left of the couch was shreds of material and the whiteboard was snapped in half.

"Oh no, that's terrible," squeaked a voice behind us.

We spun round to see Pheasel and Guggernaut standing there with fake sympathetic looks on their faces.

"You did this," said Hungrabun, her little paws shaking.

"Us?" said Pheasel pretending to look shocked. "How could you even suggest such a thing? Why, Guggernaut and I were just going to our next match and thought we'd pop in on the way to wish you good luck. Right, Guggernaut?"

Guggernaut looked confused. "I thought you said we were going to pop in and smash up their dressing room?"

Pheasel rolled his eyes. "No… That wasn't us, remember? We got here and it was already like this.

REMEMBER?"

Guggernaut screwed up his face in thought. "Right … yeah … I remember now. You said we'd smash up their room but tell them we didn't. I remember now, boss."

Pheasel closed his eyes and rubbed his temple. "You're hard work sometimes, Guggernaut, you really are."

"We'll report you for this," I said.

"I bet they'll disqualify you from the tournament," added Max.

"Oh yeah?" snapped Pheasel. "And just who exactly is going to be the one to tell Guggernaut that he's out? Even if people weren't terrified of upsetting him, we're the stars of this tournament. When you're a star, you can get away with anything. I mean, do you really think you're the first team we've ever done this to? Anyway, we'll leave you now, I can see you have some tidying up to do. Best of luck in your match."

Pheasel and Guggernaut walked away sniggering.

Hungrabun let out a scream. "They're horrible!" she said. "Pheasel wouldn't be anything without Guggernaut. Why are you so calm?"

She was looking at Kiwi who, unusually, hadn't said a word in all this. "It's just mind games," he said. "You can't let them get in your head: that's what they want. Ask yourself, why would they do this?"

Hungrabun threw up her paws. "Because they're the worst?"

"Because they're scared," said Max. "Or Pheasel is at least."

"Scared of us?" said Hungrabun.

"Of course he is," I said. "He's already seen you

beat two teams no one thought you could beat. But you basically did it individually. He must be worried what will happen if you two ever figure out how to work as a team."

Hungrabun and Kiwi looked at each other.

A scary grin formed on Hungrabun's face. "Then he should prepare to be terrified," she said. "Because that's exactly what's going to happen."

"We need to get past Electric Dreams first," said Max.

Gears started turning in my head. "Hey, Kiwi, let me see those trainers again," I said. "And Hungrabun, I need to have a look at that shield…"

LEVEL 9

"Having a stadium inside a volcano is a terrible idea."

Max had a point. As we came out into the ring
by crossing a stone walkway, bursts of lava from
the surrounding moat snapped at our feet. The
spectators in the stone-carved stands around us

KIWI!

♡Marry me
Hypnohog!♡

also seemed to be a little on edge, especially those in the front row who had to keep diving out the way of splashes of molten rock.

Despite this, the crowd showed their appreciation for the Super Fluffy Animals by drowning out the roar of the volcano with their cheers. I could even see loads of creatures wearing red puffer jackets like the one Kiwi had worn in the last round.

Across the ring stood the meanest-looking toad I had ever seen. Flipswitch was green and had a yellow mohawk. Next to him was the sinister Hypnohog, dressed in a black cape and top hat.

Creepiest.

Team.

Ever.

ELECTRIC DREAMS

As the announcer began the introductions, the Super Fluffy Animals gathered for a last-minute team talk.

"All right," I said. "Hungrabun's stomach is still bothering her, so we're going to have to play this one smart. Everyone's clear on the plan?"

Hungrabun and Kiwi nodded.

"Are you sure this is going to work?" Max asked me, sidestepping a splash of lava.

"Definitely," I said. Possibly, I thought. "The key is to work as a team. Do that and we'll be unstoppable. Now, who's going first?"

"Kiwi is," said Hungrabun.

"… Super Fluffy Animals!" yelled the announcer, signalling it was time to get things started. Seconds later, the bell rang and Kiwi squared off against Hypnohog.

Hypnohog's main skill was his ability to hypnotise his opponents. With our TV wrecked we hadn't been able to watch his last match ourselves, but we had received word that he had managed to mesmerize the members of the other team into fighting each other, while he and Flipswitch drank smoothies and played cards.

"Remember to avoid eye contact," I shouted, ducking under a lump of molten rock that flew overhead. Luckily, Kiwi was a step ahead of me. At the first sign of Hypnohog trying to meet his gaze, Kiwi was gone. Moments later Hypnohog tumbled to the ground as Kiwi barged into him from behind. The boar then sprang to his feet but Kiwi had already vanished. This sequence repeated itself several times, with the crowd cheering more and more wildly.

A frustrated Hypnohog looked close to breaking, until I saw a glint in his eye. "I really like your shoes," he said.

"You do?" said Kiwi, reappearing. "They're pretty cool, aren't they? I got them from the stall backstage."

"Kiwi, no!" the three of us yelled, but it was too late. Eye contact had been made.

"You are under my spell," said the boar, waving his trotters in the air as his eyes spun round and round.

"OK," I said, looking at Hungrabun. "No need to panic. We just have to move to plan B."

Hungrabun nodded and took off the shiny shield she had bought from the stall. "Let's hope your idea works," she said, flinging the shield into the ring. "Hey, Kiwi, catch!"

Thankfully the hypnosis hadn't completely

taken hold yet, and Kiwi still had the awareness to catch the shield. Perhaps it was the concentration required to put someone under, but at first Hypnohog didn't seem to notice that he was no longer looking into Kiwi's eyes. Instead, he was looking into his own eyes in the reflection of the shield.

Moments later, Kiwi peered out from behind the shield at Hypnohog, who was just standing there, swaying slightly.

"Are you all right?" asked Kiwi.

"How can I obey you?" he replied in a strange monotonous voice.

Kiwi scratched his head. "Well, I suppose it would help us if you just … went home?"

"As you command," replied Hypnohog, and off he went.

"Where are you going?" yelled Flipswitch. "You can't just leave me."

But that's exactly what Hypnohog did, quickly making his way out of the ring and then the arena. An enraged Flipswitch came forward and fired her tongue at Kiwi, whipping it halfway across the ring. Kiwi reacted just in time, bringing up the shield. Flipswitch's tongue made a thwack sound as it stuck to the metal, before snapping back, snatching the shield from Kiwi's wings.

"You won't be needing this," she said, flinging the metallic disc out of the ring and into the molten lava.

"Hey, that was mine!" yelled Hungrabun.

Flipswitch wasn't about to apologize though. She whipped her tongue at Kiwi again, this time catching him on his right wing. Kiwi tried to pull away, but the grip was too tight.

"Oh no," said Max. "She's going to use her shock attack."

"That's what we're counting on," I said. I just hoped I had got this right.

We watched as sparks flew from Flipswitch's mouth, travelling along her tongue and into Kiwi, at which point … nothing happened.

"Phew! That didn't hurt a bit." Kiwi grinned.

"Flo, you were right!" said Max.

After examining Kiwi's shoes backstage I
realized that the soles were made of rubber.
I had once helped my mum fix her computer
and I remembered having to wear these special
wristbands that stopped static electricity from
damaging the circuits. Following the same principle
I guessed that Kiwi's rubber soles would be enough
to stop electricity from passing through him.

*Video Game Tip: Just to be clear, trainers wouldn't be
enough to stop you getting electrocuted in the real
world. Fortunately, you're also unlikely to encounter
any giant toads with electric tongues in the real
world. If you do … er … check with an adult?*

Flipswitch's face was a mixture of confusion and
fear. After a few seconds of not knowing what to
do next, it seemed to dawn on her that she had

other moves at her disposal. She flicked her tongue, flinging Kiwi high into the air, then bringing him crashing down on to the mat.

Then she did it again.

And again.

And again.

The fourth time, the impact was enough to break Flipswitch's grip as Kiwi tumbled free, landing inches from Hungrabun.

Kiwi sat up, rubbing his head. "OK, that DID hurt a bit," he said as he tagged her in.

"You're going to regret hurting my friend," Hungrabun told Flipswitch, as she slipped into Kiwi's trainers.

"She called me friend," grinned Kiwi as Max and I helped him to his feet.

"Not as much as you're going to regret tagging

in," said Flipswitch to Hungrabun, whipping her tongue at the bunny, wrapping it round her left paw. Again she tried her shock attack and again, thanks to the trainers, it failed. To emphasize the point Hungrabun slammed a foot down on Flipswitch's tongue.

Flipswitch let out a yell as her tongue wrapped back into her mouth.

And then things happened very quickly.

An enraged Flipswitch fired her tongue at Hungrabun.

Hungrabun opened her jaws.

Flipswitch, realizing she was about to have her tongue bitten off, snapped it back.

Her tongue pulled a small boat out of Hungrabun's stomach.

Flipswitch did not get out of the way in time.

BLAAAAAAAMMMMMMM!!!

As everyone stared in shocked silence at the boat lying on top of Flipswitch in the middle of the ring, the bell rang.

"We did it!" yelled Kiwi, running to hug Hungrabun. Max and I joined them in the ring to celebrate.

"Your winners, and advancing to the finals ..." shouted the announcer, "... the ..."

The crowd, although fortunately not the volcano itself, erupted.

"SUPER
FLUFFY
ANIMALS!"

"Now, let's bring out the team they're going to be facing in the finals," continued the announcer. "Let's hear it for Guggernaut and Pheasel."

The boos were deafening as Guggernaut and Pheasel made their way to the ring, neither of them looking particularly pleased.

"Pheasel, would you like to say a few words about your upcoming match?" asked the announcer.

Pheasel snatched the microphone. "All you people take a good look at your favourites, the Super Fluffy Animals. Because this is the last time you'll ever see them in once piece."

The boos from the crowd intensified. The announcer waited for them to die down before handing the mic to Kiwi. "Strong words there, Kiwi. Anything you'd like to add?"

"Yeah," said Kiwi. "We got something to say. These

guys think they can bully everyone. We're not afraid of them. Come the final we're going—"

But Kiwi was unable to finish his sentence as Guggernaut crashed into his back, sending him flying across the ring. Hungrabun too was nailed from behind by Pheasel, knocking her to the ground. The crowd gasped in shock.

Pheasel and Guggernaut stood over Kiwi and Hungrabun's helpless bodies and laughed.

"Final?" whispered Pheasel. "Oh, I don't think you're making the final."

LEVEL 10

"Whoops!" said Pheasel. "How clumsy of us, walking into you both like that. Oh, I do hope we haven't accidentally hurt you."

I charged into Pheasel, knocking him to the ground. Suddenly, the ring filled up with creatures from backstage. Hands grabbed at me, pulling me off Pheasel before I had the chance to get revenge for what they had just done to Hungrabun and Kiwi.

Before I knew what was happening, the four of us were backstage. Kiwi and Hungrabun, motionless after the attack, had been carried off by several creatures – part of the backstage staff by the looks of it. They had struggled with her, which wasn't surprising given the mountain of items in her stomach.

"Those two are in pretty bad shape," Shilla said to the staff. "Get them in the van. See that they get the help they need."

"We're coming too," I said as the Super Fluffy Animals were helped into a large red van.

"Of course," said Shilla.

Moments later we were shooting out of the arena, leaving the volcano behind. Max and I watched our team, lying flat out on a stretcher. Both of them looked rough, but Kiwi looked especially bad. He seemed to be drifting in and out of consciousness.

"Don't worry, guys," I said. "It's going to be OK. Right, Max?"

Max looked at me uncertainly. "Yeah … of course," he said.

"Can't … believe … those creeps … sucker-punched … us like that," wheezed Hungrabun.

"Just take it easy," I told her, putting a hand on her shoulder. "We'll be at the hospital soon."

A few minutes later the van came to a stop and its door swung open. Shilla was just getting off a buggy.

"Here we are then," she said

Max and I stepped out first, on to a crystal road surrounded by glistening towers made from diamonds, rubies and emeralds. Light seemed to dance through the buildings and fill up the sky with all the colours of the rainbow.

The city was amazing, but there was something missing.

"So where's the hospital?" I asked.

"A what?" asked Shilla. "A hop-spittal, did you say?"

Max and I smiled, thinking she must be joking. A few seconds passed and Shilla's blank expression remained.

"It's a building where you go when you're not feeling well," said Max. "They make you better there."

Shilla still looked clueless. "Hmm. That does sound useful," she admitted. "I'm afraid there's nothing like that here."

"But you said that they were going to get the help they needed," I said.

"Yes, to get to the next arena," she said, pointing towards a giant blue structure behind us. I instantly recognized it as the Sapphire Stadium. "I didn't think it would be a good idea to transport them in the buggies, given their condition."

"Given their condition?" repeated Max, looking as dumbstruck as I felt. "Surely given their condition, the final can't go ahead?"

"Or it should be delayed at least, until they've healed," I added. I agreed with Max that the team were too hurt to fight right now, but we couldn't forget that them winning the tournament was our only shot at getting home.

Shilla looked even more lost. "Delay the final? That'd be ... unheard of."

"Like hospitals, apparently," I muttered.

"Yeah, like hops-it-alls," she said. "If you don't show up for the final, I'm afraid it would be considered a forfeit."

"What about the two cheats who attacked them?"

I said. "Why haven't they been disqualified?"

"Pheasel and Guggernaut are claiming it was an accident," she said. "We've reviewed the video footage and it really is quite difficult to say definitively, so…" She held up her hands as if there wasn't anything else she could add.

"That's ridiculous," I said. "You're clearly just too scared to punish them."

Shilla raised her nose. "I don't know what you mean."

"I think … I'm going to … be sick," said Hungrabun, struggling to sit up.

"My sentiments exactly," I said, wagging a finger at Shilla.

"No. I mean. I think. I'm actually going. To be sick," said Hungrabun.

"Come on then. We don't want a mess out here.

I'll take you to your dressing room," said Shilla.

Max and I carried the stretcher with the Super Fluffy Animals on it, grumbling the entire way – partly due to the injustice of the situation and partly because of how heavy Hungrabun was. I was surprised to discover our dressing room was still in one piece this time.

Hungrabun's face was growing greener by the

second. All we could hope was that we'd get her to the toilet in time.

"I'll leave you to it then," said Shilla, who clearly hoped to make it out of the room before the throwing up started.

Unfortunately, no one got what they hoped for.

Max and I managed to get ourselves and Kiwi behind the couch in time. Shilla wasn't so lucky.

BLEEEEEUUUUUUURP

We peeked out from behind our barricade.

Shilla was drenched and shaking. I thought she might cry but she held herself together, appeared to count to ten, then said through gritted teeth, "I. Will. Come. And. Collect. You. Soon."

She slammed the door behind her.

"Hungrabun, are you OK?" I said, rushing over to her. Not getting too close though. There was a lot of puke.

"I am," she said, sounding surprised. "You know what, I actually feel much better. I think my stomach is finally cleared."

"Flo, have you seen this?" asked Max.

I followed his gaze across the room. There in the

126

RRRGGGGGHHHHHH!!!

corner, dripping wet, were Morpher and Camo, the Shapeshifters. Bizarrely, they were still in their giant hand and arrow forms.

"You've really got to learn to digest your food," came a weak voice.

"Kiwi, you're awake!" said Hungrabun.

Kiwi flinched, grabbing his head. "Sore though," he said. "Those two got us pretty good, huh?"

Hungrabun put her paw on his shoulder. "Yeah," she said.

"We'll just have to hit them back even harder when we face them," said Kiwi.

"Face them?" said Hungrabun. "Kiwi, look at you, you're in no state to go out there."

Kiwi waved her away. "Don't worry, I'll be fine," he said, sitting up and promptly falling off the stretcher.

As Max and Hungrabun helped Kiwi up, a thought flashed across my mind. "Hungrabun, your health vial!" I said.

"Yes!" shouted Max, making Kiwi flinch. "The one you got after the first match," he said, softly this time.

Hungrabun looked down at the floor. "I got a red one, remember?" she said. "More health for me, but no one else can use it."

"Oh," I said quietly. "I forgot about that."

Hungrabun looked like she was about to cry. "If I hadn't been so selfish…"

"Don't be like that," said Kiwi. "I mean, I did buy myself a coat after all. I miss that coat."

Max's face lit up. "Guys! We still have credits from the last match."

"Holy Pac-Man, you're right," I said. "We can just go get more health vials."

"You two go," said Max. "I'll stay here with Kiwi."

I looked at Max suspiciously. "You sure you don't just want to examine those Shapeshifters over there?"

Max grinned at me. "No harm in looking, is there? They're still in the same shapes they were in when Hungrabun ate them. What's that all about?"

"Mmm," I said. "I'll admit that is a bit weird. See what you can find out then."

Hungrabun and I left him to it. We quickly found the stall along the corridor.

"Two of your strongest health vials, please," said Hungrabun to the penguin behind the counter.

"Sorry, we're fresh out," she said.

"What? Red and blue?" asked Hungrabun.

"Afraid so," the penguin replied. "The big fella and the ratty-looking one were just here, grabbed my last two."

"Guggernaut and Pheasel," I said. "Those sneaks. They knew we'd be needing them."

Hungrabun looked up at me. "You know what this means?" she said.

I nodded.

"I'll have to face them by myself," she said.

"You sure?" I asked. As much as I wanted to go home, I didn't want to see Hungrabun hurt.

She nodded. "My entire life everyone told me I was too small to compete in the Battles. But here I am in the final. This is my dream, Flo, and I've come too far to let those bullies stop me. Does that make sense?"

"I think so," I said. "It's like when I got the number

one rank on Last to Leave. Even though it's like the hardest Battle Royale game on the planet I knew I had it in me to be the best at it, so I didn't stop until I was."

Video Game Tip: Battle Royale games involve lots of players in a contained area fighting to be the last person or team standing. Some of them involve dancing, for some reason.

"I didn't really understand any of that," said Hungrabun.

"It doesn't matter," I said. "The point is I know you can do it. And you won't be by yourself. You'll have me in your corner."

"You can't actually fight though," she reminded me.

"Yeah, but I can shout insults at the other team,"

I said. "I'm really good at it."

Hungrabun smiled. "Better than nothing," she said. She looked up at the stand. "I suppose we should get something else then. I'll take another shield. I lost my last one, and I think I might need one against Guggernaut's attacks. And for Kiwi…"

She pointed towards an item at the back of the stand. "What do you think?" she grinned.

I laughed. "Yeah, that's sooo Kiwi."

"I'll take it," she said.

LEVEL 11

When a now (mostly) clean Shilla came to fetch us for the finals, I told Max to stay behind and make sure Kiwi didn't come out. Kiwi was furious, but I knew it was the right thing to do.

It was a long march to the ring with Hungrabun. Neither of us said anything. What was there to say? For me and Max, everything was riding on Hungrabun beating an undefeated, ruthless team by herself. I didn't see any point in telling Hungrabun this though. After our conversation earlier I was in no doubt she'd do everything she could to beat those two.

But it was hard not to think about how small her chances seemed.

As we reached a set of crystal doors leading to the main arena, instead of pushing them open Hungrabun booted them down with her tiny feet.

The place went nuts with chanting.

HUNGRA-BUN!

WE WANT KIWI

KIWI

S-F-A
S-F-A **S-F-A**
S-F-A
S-F-A

We walked towards the ring down a (literal) emerald aisle, surrounded by stands made of shimmering blue crystal and overflowing with excited creatures. The Sapphire Stadium was the grandest and most famous of all the Critter Clash arenas, reserved for the biggest matches. It sent shivers down my spine to see it this close up. If Hungrabun was intimidated by it all, it didn't show.

What did show was her anger when she caught sight of Guggernaut and Pheasel waiting in the ring with the ref and the announcer. She growled, before breaking into a run. I had to chase after her to avoid being left behind.

"Sound the bell," demanded Hungrabun as she hit the ring.

"I haven't even introduced you yet," said the announcer, looking outraged.

Hungrabun snarled at him. "Then make it quick!"

The announcer's face turned white. "In the red corner, Guggernaut and Pheasel. In the blue corner, Hungrabun and … er…"

"Just me," said Hungrabun, to smirks from Guggernaut and Pheasel.

"Just Hungrabun," said the announcer, before getting out of there.

"Hungrabun, what's your plan?" I asked.

She didn't reply. Instead she gave me a grin, licking her lips.

I looked over at the giant growling monster that was Guggernaut. Hungrabun was going to have a hard time keeping that meal down.

The bell rang and Guggernaut charged towards us. But Hungrabun charged too, meeting him in the middle. As Guggernaut's momentum carried him forward, Hungrabun slid right under him, coming to a stop in front of Pheasel. She jumped on to him, grabbing hold of lumps of his brown fur.

"Hey! Get off, get off," moaned Pheasel. "Guggernaut, help me!"

A confused Guggernaut was at the other end of the ring, right in front of me, wondering where Hungrabun had gone. At Pheasel's shout he turned, spotted Hungrabun and charged. At the last second, Hungrabun dived out of the way in time to watch Guggernaut smash into Pheasel, sending him flying into the third row.

Guggernaut let out a roar. He marched towards Hungrabun.

"Move!" I yelled at her.

But she didn't go anywhere, standing her ground instead. Guggernaut raised a giant fist and brought it smashing down. A huge clang echoed around the stadium as Hungrabun brought her shield up in time to catch the blow.

Unfazed, Guggernaut swung one of his other fists at her, but again it was Hungrabun's shield that took the brunt of the blow. Guggernaut started hammering her, swinging all four arms in rotation, dropping punch after punch. The shield was holding up, but it was clear from the dents that were forming rapidly in its surface that this couldn't last much longer.

Hungrabun didn't seem to be panicking though. Her eyes were darting back and forth between the shield above her and Guggernaut's right leg. She was waiting for something. An opening, maybe.

Seconds later I was proved right. After a barrage of punches, Guggernaut took a breather. As he wiped sweat off his brow, Hungrabun slipped out from underneath her shield and launched herself into the air, feet first, knocking him off balance and dropping him on his butt. It was the ...

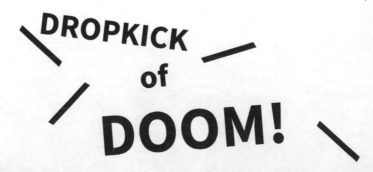

DROPKICK of DOOM!

"I taught her that!" I yelled to the crowd.

But Hungrabun wasn't finished, taking advantage of the startled Guggernaut by sinking her teeth into his leg.

AAAAARRRRRGGGGGGHHHHHHHHHHHH!!!

Guggernaut continued to scream as he tried to shake Hungrabun off, with no success. The crowd was going wild as it seemed the tables had finally turned on Guggernaut and Pheasel.

Pheasel. I realized I'd forgotten about him. I looked over to the stands where he had landed but there was no sign of him. And that's when a furry arm grabbed me round the neck.

"Hey, Hungrabun," shouted Pheasel. "Let go or your coach gets it."

"No, Hungrabun!" I cried, but it was too late. Hungrabun had already released Guggernaut and was heading towards us.

"Pheasel, enough of that! Back in your own corner," ordered the ref.

I reached up and grabbed hold of Pheasel's arm, then tossed him over my head.

"Hungrabun, I'm fine," I yelled. "Watch out!"

My warning came too late as all four of Guggernaut's arms struck at once, blasting Hungrabun in the back and knocking her to the ground.

Pheasel let out a horrible laugh as Guggernaut began to slowly circle the floored Hungrabun. She managed to raise her head slightly, looking towards me. Her eyes struggled to focus as she mouthed the words 'I'm sorry' at me.

No! It couldn't end like this. Then I remembered Hungrabun's health potion. I reached into the pockets of my coach jacket and pulled out … nothing. It wasn't there.

There was a cackle from the other end of the ring. Pheasel was standing there waving a red vial at me. "Looking for something?" He laughed.

He must have picked my pocket when he grabbed me. "Give it back," I yelled pointlessly. I thought about chasing after him but knew there wasn't time. Guggernaut was one blow away from winning. It really was over.

A finger tapped me on the shoulder. Instinctively I grabbed it, ready to throw its owner as far as I could.

"Flo, stop! It's me!"

"Max?" I said, spinning round to find my friend looking terrified. Behind him were the giant arrow and disembodied hand that were the Shapeshifters, both pointing into the ring. "Sorry! I didn't realize it was you. What are you doing here? Why are they here? Where's Kiwi?"

"That's what I came to tell you," he said. "I got a bit caught up examining the Shapeshifters. When I remembered to check on Kiwi, I realized he was gone."

"Gone?" I said. "Gone where?"

"I don't know," he said, shrugging. "But Flo, about the Shapeshifters. I think I've found something important. Something you need to know. It's about—"

"Look!" I yelled, pointing to the ring.

The crowd saw it too, and their reaction blew the roof off the place. Or would have done if it had one.

Standing in the middle of the ring, right behind Guggernaut, was a wobbly Kiwi.

Guggernaut and Pheasel glanced at each other then burst out laughing.

"Look who's showed up to stop you, Guggernaut," said Pheasel.

"Ha ha!" laughed Guggernaut.

"You've got it wrong, Pheasel," said Kiwi. "I'm not here to stop you. I'm here to be with my friend. If the Super Fluffy Animals are going down, then they'll go down together. Because we're a team."

Hungrabun and Kiwi smiled at each other.

Pheasel looked disgusted. "You mean you're here knowing you're going to lose? How honourable. But also sickening. Go on then, Guggernaut. Give him what he wants."

As Guggernaut cracked his knuckles, Kiwi held up a wing. "Wait one second," he pleaded. He reached into his feathers and took out a pair of dark sunglasses. Then he grinned at Hungrabun. "A friend got me these. She thought I'd like them. If I'm going to lose, I'm going to lose looking good. Do you mind?"

Guggernaut thought about it then shrugged. "No difference to me," he said. "You won't look good after I've finished with you."

"Thanks," said Kiwi as he slipped the glasses on to his face.

"Got to admit, he does look good in them," I sighed.

Guggernaut raised his fists

and then swung all four
of them at Kiwi. Just
as they were about
to connect, a bright
yellow laser fired out
of the sunglasses,

striking
Guggernaut on the chest,
sending him flying out of the ring.

After a momentary stunned silence, the crowd
was on their feet – those who had them.

Kiwi took off the sunglasses. "Wow. Did not know
they did that," he said. "Nice pick, Hungrabun!"

With Guggernaut unconscious outside the
ring, all eyes turned towards Pheasel. He smiled

nervously. "Hey … er … maybe we can talk about this?" he said, backing away slowly. But Max and I had already made our way round the ring, one from each side, blocking him from going anywhere. Pheasel stumbled, landing on his butt, and two health vials tumbled out of his fur. A red one and a blue one.

The red one belonged to Hungrabun. I tossed it to her, and after drinking its contents, she immediately popped up, raring to go. Remembering that the blue vials could be used by anybody, I chucked the other one to Kiwi, who also perked up after consuming it.

There was just one thing left to do. Max and I grabbed Pheasel and threw him into the ring. Hungrabun's mouth opened wide and swallowed him whole.

The bell rang.

"YOUR WINNERS FOR THIS YEAR!"

screamed the announcer.

"HUNGRABUN AND KIWI — THE SUPER FLUFFY ANIMALS!"

The cheering from the crowd was the loudest I'd ever heard. Confetti rained from the sky as the four of us danced around in celebration.

"Ugh," said Hungrabun. "Actually, you know what? That last thing I ate is very disagreeable. **PTOOOO!**"

She spat out Pheasel and he flew through the air, landing in a heap next to Guggernaut, who happened to be waking up just at that moment.

"This is all your fault," a dripping-wet Pheasel screamed at his partner. "Biggest mistake I ever made was teaming up with a loser like you!"

Guggernaut held out a hand and flicked his finger at Pheasel, smashing him through the arena wall.

"This is the greatest moment of my life," said Hungrabun.

"Mine too," said Kiwi.

Pausing in my celebrations, I looked at Max. "We're still here," I said to him. "But we completed the game. What more is there to do?"

Kiwi must have overheard me. "Oh, there's tons more to do," he said.

"Yeah," said Hungrabun. "This isn't the end of the Super Fluffy Animals. It's just the beginning."

"What do you mean?" I asked.

"This was just a regional tournament," said Kiwi. "If we want to be Grand Champions there's sectionals, nationals, internationals…"

"Don't forget interplanetaries and interdimensionals," said Hungrabun.

"How could I?" laughed Kiwi.

My heart sank. We weren't going anywhere for a very, very long time.

LEVEL 12

"Flo, this is what I wanted to talk to you about," said Max. "I think there might be another way out of the game."

"What are you talking about?" I asked.

"I was examining the Shapeshifters," he said. "I had the TV on watching Hungrabun and noticed that wherever she moved on the screen, the two of them would point towards her."

I shrugged. "They're bugged, we already know this," I said. "They can't do anything else now but point at Hungrabun."

"No, it's more than that. Watch," said Max. He turned to Morpher, the floating hand, and asked her, "Are you trying to tell us something?"

The hand turned itself round, making a thumbs-up gesture.

"Are you trying to tell us how to get home?" asked Max.

Morpher once again gave us the thumbs up.

"What do we have to do to get home?" asked Max.

Morpher and Camo both pointed at Hungrabun.

"I think we have to let Hungrabun eat us again," said Max.

As the hands changed shape to show their approval, Hungrabun looked a little freaked out. "You want me to do what now?" she demanded.

"How is that going to help?" I asked.

"I think there's something inside Hungrabun that

we can use to get out," said Max.

Another thumbs up.

Max was on to something. Someone was clearly trying to send us a message. Then I remembered something I had forgotten.

"There WAS a bug with this version of the game," I said. "More than that – it was an exploit."

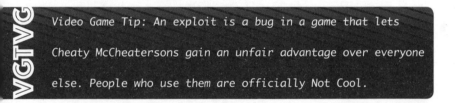

Video Game Tip: An exploit is a bug in a game that lets Cheaty McCheatersons gain an unfair advantage over everyone else. People who use them are officially Not Cool.

"It let you control certain characters – actually control them, not just coach them. You had to be a proper genius to get it to work though, and of course they fixed it in later versions."

"We know a proper genius," said Max.

We looked at Morpher and Camo.

"Mum?" I said.

The thumb went up again.

I let out a gasp. "All right then," I said. "Hungrabun, it's been a pleasure.

But Max and I need to leave now. And apparently the way to do that is via your stomach."

Hungrabun looked conflicted about what to do. "Well, I mean, I don't want you to go… But I am a bit peckish…"

"You're leaving?" said Kiwi. "Now? But we've still got so much more to do. What'll we do without you?"

"You'll both be OK," said Max. "You've got each other now. No one's going to be able to stop the Super Fluffy Animals."

"Yeah … and to be honest, after the Dropkick of Doom I'm not really sure there's much more I can teach you," I said. "I can honestly say you're the best team we've ever coached."

Kiwi threw his wings round our ankles. "I'm going to miss you guys," he said.

"Me too," said Hungrabun. "Thanks for everything. And please don't leave a mess in my tummy."

"We won't," I said.

Hungrabun nodded, took a deep breath and swallowed us whole.

And we were back where we had started, inside her cavernous stomach with its pink fleshy walls. It was still full of junk, which was surprising given the amount of vomit earlier.

"She's worried about us making a mess?" I muttered.

"Not sure what we're looking for," said Max. "It could be any of these things."

I shook my head. "No," I said. "I'll bet any money it's that."

I pointed at the swirling gooey hole in the middle of her stomach.

"The wall glitch?" asked Max.

"I don't think that's what it is any more," I said.

Max didn't look convinced. "Well, if you're wrong,

we'll spend the rest of time falling into a black hole."

"Trust me," I said. "Have I ever led you astray before?"

"We've been over this, Flo," said Max. "The answer is yes. Always yes."

"Come on," I said, reaching out to him. "It'll be fine."

Max sighed and took my hand. We stepped into the hole. The last thing we saw was:

BONUS LEVEL

We were on an aeroplane. Us and about a hundred other people by the looks of things.

"Another game," yelled Max above the deafening roar of the engine, the frustration clear on his face.

"Another game," I repeated, sharing his disappointment.

I had assumed that Mum must have somehow figured out a way to add a portal to Critter Clash. I had hoped it would lead us back to the real world, but clearly not. We were back at square one.

I looked around the cabin. The other passengers

were a colourful bunch, each one with their own unique look, costume and hairstyle. That likely meant these were all real people, since real people generally spent time getting their characters to look the way they wanted them.

Then it hit me what game we were in. "Max, this is Last to Leave," I said. "It's a Battle Royale game."

At that moment, a passenger caught my eye and I almost fell over. Max had to keep me upright.

"What is it?" he asked.

There were two possibilities. The first: it was just coincidence that someone had made a character look like that.

Then there was the second possibility.

I pointed across the cabin.

When Max saw the passenger, it was his turn to almost fall over.

The woman had seen us and was waving. "Flo, it's me!" she yelled. "I'm here in the game. I've come to save—"

She was cut off when the plane door opened. Several people got up at once and rushed towards the exit.

Mum didn't get out of the way in time. Some of the other players bumped into her, knocking her backwards out of the open door.

She was gone.

To be continued...

LEVEL UP!

UP!

LAST ONE
STANDING

**COMING SOON TO
A BOOKSHOP NEAR YOU!**

TURN THE PAGE FOR A SNEAK PEEK AT FLO AND MAX'S NEXT ADVENTURE...

LEVEL 1

My mum had just fallen out of an aeroplane. How's your day going?

To be honest, things like this had become quite normal for me and my best friend Max, ever since the two of us found ourselves trapped inside a series of video games. So far we had been space soldiers, block people and creature coaches. But it had always been just the two of us trapped in the games.

Until now.

The latest game we had jumped into was Last

to Leave – the world's most intense Battle Royale survival game – and for reasons currently known only to her, Mum had joined us. I'd have asked her why, but as I mentioned, **SHE HAD JUST FALLEN OUT OF AN AEROPLANE**.

"Flo, what are we going to do?" yelled Max above the roar of the plane's engine and the noise from the other players.

"We need to go after her," I said, grabbing hold of his arm.

"And how do we do that? By jumping out of the plane?" He began to laugh, but stopped when he saw my expression. "You can't be serious!" he shouted.

I looked him straight in the eye. "Max," I said. "You've known me all your life. Does jumping out of a plane sound like something I'd try to get you to do?"

Max considered this for a second. "Well, yes, it does actually."

"Exactly," I said. "So, stop wasting time. Besides, you've got a parachute on."

"Do I?" he said, looking over his shoulder. "Oh yeah. Where did that come from?"

"I don't know," I said. "Everyone just gets one."

Getting to the front of the plane wasn't proving as easy as I had hoped, given the urgency of the situation. A blockade of players had formed as they all lined up to jump out. I elbowed and pushed my way past them until Max and I were at the door, but when I scanned the island below us I couldn't see any sign of Mum.

I turned to Max, whose eyes were like giant saucers. Normally this would be the point when I'd try to calm him down, give him some encouragement and tell him everything was going to be OK. But that would take time we didn't have. The longer we left it, the further we'd be from Mum and the harder it would be to find her. So I did the only thing I could do.

I shoved Max out of the plane. And following the sound of his screams, I dived after him.

I should probably have told him how to open his parachute.

As we plummeted towards the ground, I used the time to remind myself of the Last to Leave map. In the north were the snow-covered mountain peaks of the Arctic Zone. The green trees of the Jungle Zone lay to the west and in the south were the sand dunes of the Desert Zone. Green hills and meadows formed the Grasslands to the east and in the centre of the map, where we were headed, were the quaint cottages and picturesque villages of the Olde Zone.

I was worried at seeing all the other players landing in positions around the map. Last to Leave was a battle to survive. Only one team could win.

With the ground racing towards us, I pulled the cord on my parachute, slowing my fall. Moments later I was relieved to see Max open his own chute. I'd known he'd figure it out! I was slightly less relieved when he proceeded to fly right into a clock tower. "OW!" I heard him yell.

I landed in the middle of the village square and my parachute vanished, as video game parachutes tend to do. I looked up at Max, who was dangling helplessly about six metres above the ground, his parachute caught in the tower's spire.

"Max, release your parachute," I shouted.

"How do I do that?" he asked.

Parachutes usually disappeared once players hit the ground. If you got stuck, you could press the X key to cut yourself free but that wasn't an option here. "Is there a button or something on the chute you could press?" I asked. "Some kind of catch maybe?"

"Not that I can see," he said. "Also, if I do get free, I'm not super keen on the massive drop that comes afterwards."

"One problem at a time, please, Max," I said, looking around the square for inspiration. But while the cobblestone streets and quiet shops and cafes looked positively charming, they didn't really offer much in the way of a solution to Max's problem.

So, in a way, it was handy when the lasers started firing.

Pew-pew!

The blast cut right through Max's chute and he dropped like a rock, straight into my open arms. This was a video game though, so unlike a rock he weighed nothing at all.

"Thanks," he said.

Another blast shot past my head, then suddenly four more players were in the square with us. Two boys and two girls, all wielding impossibly large laser cannons. Pointed our way.

"We'd better go," I said.

"I was thinking that," agreed Max.

I started sprinting across the square, shots nipping at my heels as I ran.

"You could put me down," yelled Max.

"No time," I shouted back.

I ran through the open doorway of a run down post

office and kicked the door shut before dumping Max on the ground.

"Come on, we need to find the back exit," I said. "They won't be long."

I was right. I had just lifted up the serving hatch of the post-office counter when the front door burst open. A mean-looking boy with neon-green spiky hair, wearing desert camouflage trousers and a white tank top, stepped inside.

"Hiding in the post office, eh?" He laughed. "Well, I've got a special delivery for you right here."

He raised his laser cannon and opened fire. Max and I dived behind the counter as the wall behind us exploded, leaving a huge hole.

"Oh, wow," I said. "I didn't know they'd added destructible environments to this game. Cool."

"I'm not sure this is the time to be admiring the

game's new features," said Max.

"Good point," I said. "Though with any luck it might give us a way out of here. Listen!"

A **click-clack** sound was coming from the other end of the room.

"He's reloading," I said. "Let's go."

Max and I sprang to our feet then dived through the hole. It brought us out into a narrow alley.

"Which way?" asked Max.

His question was quickly answered when another member of the attacking squad appeared at the end of the alley – a girl this time, wearing dark sunglasses and a full-length purple coat.

"Run, little bunnies, run," she cackled.

We took her advice and ran in the opposite direction, then turned right into a lane and headed along a row of back gardens.

"In here," I said, opening the third gate we reached. As Max pushed past me into the garden, I glanced up the lane but there was no one there. Yet. I closed the gate, then Max and I headed into the house and went straight upstairs, each step squeaking beneath us as if they were trying to give us away. We entered what was clearly a nursery, with a cot and pictures of balloons and teddy bears on the walls. Carefully, we crept towards the window. There wasn't much to see beyond a few more similar-looking houses and a small garage sandwiched between them. Carmack's Cars.

Max was about to speak when I held up my hand and we moved away from the window. I could hear footsteps outside.

"Where'd they go?" asked the girl we had seen in the alley.

"Dunno," replied the boy from the post office. "But they can't have got far."

"They might have found equipment by now," said a new voice, another girl. "Weapons even. We should bounce."

"You're right," said a fourth voice. "And look, we've got wheels."

I chanced a peek out of the window. He was right. There in the garage was an open-top truck. Vehicles were invaluable in this game so it was a shame we hadn't got to it first, but I couldn't help feeling relieved as the four of them climbed into the truck, two in the cab at the front and two riding in the back with an assortment of wooden crates.

"It's OK, we're safe," I said as the truck pulled out of the garage and turned on to the lane. Max breathed a long sigh as he looked out of the window.

Then we saw her.

Crouching down, hidden from the other team behind the crates, was Mum. Travelling further away by the second.

ABOUT THE AUTHOR

Tom Nicoll has been writing since he was in school, where he enjoyed trying to fit in as much silliness in his essays as he could possibly get away with. When not writing, he enjoys playing video games (especially the ones where he gets beaten by kids half his age from all over the world). He is also a big comedy, TV and movie nerd. Tom lives just outside Edinburgh with his wife and two daughters.

LEVEL UP: BEAST BATTLES

is his eleventh book for children.

ABOUT THE ILLUSTRATOR

Anjan Sarkar first realized he loved illustration as a child when, with a few strokes of a crayon, he drew a silly face that made his mum laugh. Silly faces are funny and make people laugh, he thought. Since then, he's grown up into a hairy-faced man who draws silly faces for a living (not just for his mum). When he's not drawing he likes walking in the countryside and eating biscuits (sometimes he does both at the same time). Anjan lives in Sheffield with his wife and two kids.

FIND OUT HOW FLO AND MAX STARTED THEIR ADVENTURES IN...